ZAYDA WAS A
COWBOY

Publication of this book was made possible by gifts from

Frieda and Melvin Dow, Houston

Glen Rosenbaum, Houston

Shirley and Bruce Stein, Houston

Gail and Gary Swartz, Houston

Mimi and Leon Toubin, Brenham

who dedicate this book to

Our *zaydes* and *bubbes*
from their Texan families

And through a generous grant from

The Texas Jewish Historical Society

ZAYDA WAS A
COWBOY

June Levitt Nislick

THE JEWISH PUBLICATION SOCIETY
Philadelphia
2005 • 5765

The Jewish Publication Society
2100 Arch Street
Philadelphia, PA 19103

Composition and Design by Book Design Studio

Manufactured in the United States of America

05 06 07 08 09 10   10 9 8 7 6 5 4 3 2 1

Library of Congress Cataloging-in-Publication Data
⅃ PBK
Nislick, June Levitt.
  Zayda was a cowboy / by June Levitt Nislick.—1st ed.
    p. cm.
  Summary: When a Jewish grandfather comes to live with his son's family, he relates his experiences fleeing Eastern Europe for America, his adventures as a cowboy, and his assimilation into American culture.
  ISBN 0-8276-0817-9 (alk. paper)
  [1. Jews—Fiction. 2. Immigrants—Fiction. 3. Emigration and immigration—Fiction. 4. Cowboys—Fiction. 5. Grandfathers—Fiction. 6. West (U.S.)—History—1890–1945—Fiction. 7. Europe, Eastern—History—20th century—Fiction.] I. Title.
  PZ7.N6395Zay 2005
  [Fic]—dc22
                        2004023596

Dedicated to

Noah Benjamin Schumer
and his zayda

ACKNOWLEDGMENTS

I would like to thank my wonderful husband, Art Nislick, who said, "Just write it!"; Grace Zimel, who said, "Just submit it!"; the Mitzvah Sisters and Mensch; Irv Tobin, son of Sam; Lynn Levitt, sister-in-law, sounding board, and wise friend; and special thanks to Janet Potter, whose insights, skills, and wit made me a better writer and this a better book.

CONTENTS

PROLOGUE

The year was 1980. Fifty-two Americans were being held hostage in Iran, and President Carter's efforts to rescue them were not successful.

Everybody was talking about the dumped chemicals poisoning Love Canal, Mount Saint Helens erupted, and in outer space, Voyager 1 reached Saturn.

George Brett was the American League Most Valuable Player and Hank Aaron hit his 715th home run. The Phillies beat the Kansas City Royals 4-2 in the World Series. Pittsburgh took the Super Bowl from the L.A. Rams; the Lakers were the N.B.A. champs; and the underdog U.S. hockey team surprised the world by winning the "gold" in the Winter Olympics.

Ronald Reagan got elected president . . . John Lennon of the Beatles was shot dead . . . I drove everyone nuts singing the Doobie Brothers hit "What a Fool Believes" night and day . . . and Zayda came to live with us.

Yes . . . most of all, when I think back to that fall of 1980, I remember Zayda . . . and I remember his arrival as though it were yesterday . . .

1

The Arrival

It wasn't really cold anymore, just damp and raw, but I felt chilled and uneasy as I thought of what lay ahead. My cap was pulled down far over my ears and my wool jacket was zipped way up, but I was still uncomfortable—maybe not because of the weather, maybe because of my thoughts. Big things were about to happen in our house, and I didn't like it.

Brian, Josh, and good old Alan were horsing around in their usual way, and I would have been just as goofy on any other day—but today I had too much on my mind.

Finally the mud-splashed yellow bus rolled up to the curb and we all piled in for the trip home. There were lots of book bags slamming into ribs, legs tangling with other legs, and the collective noise was deafening; but there was nothing unusual about this. James, our regular driver, just stared straight ahead, too experienced to even try to quiet down the boys and girls. When the last one boarded, he growled, "Siddown and pipe down!" which he said every day, and we were off.

Brian asked me, "Hey, Bill, gonna meet us and shoot a few baskets later?"

"If I can. Don't know what my mother has in mind. I don't know what to expect, you know, my grandfather and all that . . ."

"Oh, yeah," Josh said. "Today's the day, right?"

I just nodded. These were my good pals, but I just didn't feel like talking about it. Brian and Josh were having a contest—who could keep pencils up his nose the longest—and I would have found them pretty amusing on any other day; but today they looked like the idiots they really were. Alan was, of course, laughing like a hyena. I smiled but didn't have my heart in it. I just didn't want my grandfather, my zayda, moving in with us, and that's the truth.

I slammed the kitchen door and was just about to drop my jacket on the floor when Mom, without turning away from the sink, shouted, "Don't drop your jacket on the floor!"

Another eyes-in-the-back-of-her-head coup for Mom.

So I hung up my coat and headed straight for the refrigerator and the orange juice. Again Mom, without turning around, said, "Not out of the pitcher. Get a glass."

"Is he here yet? Is Dad here with him?"

Mom kept her eyes on the potatoes in the pot in the sink, went on peeling, and said, "Dad dropped Zayda off a couple of hours ago and went back to the store. I think Zayda is asleep in the living room. I haven't checked in the past hour, and it's pretty quiet in there."

"Should I take a look, or what?"

Now Mom wiped her hands on her apron, shut off the cold water, sighed deeply, turned around and sat down at the kitchen table. She motioned to me to join her.

For a minute or two she just sat there, pushing crumbs around on the plastic tablecloth. Then she said, "Look . . ."

4

"Look," she began again, "this is going to be new and probably not too easy for all of us. Zayda has lived alone for many years and he will have just as hard a time getting used to us as the other way around. You know I was against it. I thought a nursing home would be better, certainly better for me; but, really, why am I going into this again? He's here and we'll just do what's necessary to make him feel comfortable and to not disrupt our lives too much. Go into the living room. If he's awake, give him a kiss and talk for a few minutes. Tell him about school. Whatever you like. If he's asleep, you can go out for the rest of the afternoon, but be home early, by five o'clock at the latest. Dad promised to be home around then, and I want us to have a nice family meal for a change. This is, I guess, an occasion. If you see Danny, make sure he comes home by five also."

Zayda is my father's father. He is old. I mean really, really old. Of course I love him. I love him the way any kid loves a very old relative he doesn't see too often. Zayda had taken care of himself in his own place ever since Bubbie died, which was quite a long time ago. In fact, I don't even remember her. Anyway, last winter Dad began getting phone calls in the middle of the night or, worse yet, in the middle of the workday. Zayda had left a burner on and set a small fire in his kitchen. Zayda had locked himself out of his apartment. Zayda had gone to buy a paper and gotten lost coming home. Stuff like that. Sometimes the calls came from Mrs. Zuckerman, who lived next door. Sometimes they came from Zayda himself. When the call came from the fire department, that was it. Mom and Dad knew they had to do something. They argued quite a bit. Once I heard, from behind their closed bedroom door, Mom's angry shouting, high-pitched and scary, and Dad repeating over and over, "But he's my father."

Finally they agreed that the best thing for Zayda was for him to move in with us.

Now that day was here. Zayda, his cartons of books and papers and photos, his clothes, and all his stuff, were here.

Mom may not have been happy, but I have to hand it to her—she certainly put on a major spread that night. And Dad gave her such a warm, loving, thankful smile from across the room. Zayda's praise ("Rosie, I never had such pot roast in my life!") and Dad's gratitude seemed to melt her a little; and Danny and I looked at each other and thought that maybe this wouldn't be so bad after all.

We told Zayda about school and sports, and he asked me if I was preparing for my bar mitzvah. I told him, "Not yet," and that was about it. Mom cleaned up. Zayda played a couple of hands of pinochle with Dad. Danny and I did our homework in front of the TV and before we knew it the first day of "Life with Zayda" was over.

We got used to Zayda pretty quickly. He was quiet. He got up early, made his own cereal and coffee, read the newspaper, and, in nice weather, took a walk around the block. He watched TV in his own room. He davened at the dining room table. I found the sight of him kind of nice, leaning over his big prayer book with its marbled end papers and red-ribbon page marker, rocking back and forth, his Hebrew rising and falling in half-melodies, the gnarled, callused index finger of his left hand moving along the columns, his skull cap always a little off center, his right hand absentmindedly stroking his wrinkled brow. At those times, he had such a sweet look on his face, it kind of choked me up a little.

Sometimes he asked us what was new but he didn't really seem interested in our answers, and we learned to just say, "Nothing, 'Zayd,'" and he didn't ask anything else. The

6

big thing was, he was there, always there. I mean, you could be picking your nose or scratching yourself and think you were all alone and—whoa—there was Zayda. But where could he go? He was—like the ancient Israelites—a "stranger in a strange land," so to speak, and I couldn't help but feel sorry for him. And I just knew he felt sorry for himself, too.

Sometimes I'd bring him a glass of tea. Yup, that's right. A *glass* of tea. And he would hold a sugar cube between his teeth and sip the tea through it, the way, he said, they did it in the old days. Anyway, I'd bring him that tea and watch him sip at it, staring into space, and I'd wonder what he was thinking, not being able to imagine anything at all.

It was most difficult for Mom. She was constantly vacuuming and picking up crumbled newspapers, and cooking and washing up. Zayda would say to Mom, "Rosie, darling, you know what I miss so much? Herring!" (Or *kreplach*. Or *kasha varnishkes*. Or something else that sounded strange and hadn't been made by anyone in our family in 50 years.) Sometimes Mom was good-natured about Zayda's cravings, and in a day or two the requested food would appear on the table, but not always. Definitely not always. By the way, Mom hated being called "Rosie," and, speaking of names, how about this? Zayda used to call me "Velvel." That's what I said. Velvel. Velvel is Yiddish for William.

"BILL. BILL!" I would shout. "My name is BILL!"

"Velvel, maybe they have a Yiddish paper at the store?"

Yeah, right. Well, the answer was no, the candy store near us did not sell Yiddish newspapers. Fortunately Dad solved that problem by getting Zayda a subscription, much to my relief.

My friends still came over sometimes, but Brian said Zayda "spooked" him, and I had to remind him that he,

Brian, had the most annoying sister in the world, and at least Zayda didn't follow us around the house butting into our conversations. Alan liked Zayda because my mom left more cookies and cake out, and Alan couldn't resist a nosh—any nosh. Mostly we went to the other guys' houses, because one thing Zayda did not like, and he made that quite clear, was our music. We got sick and tired of hearing him shout, "Shut up the noise!"

Sometimes Zayda and Dad would talk about the news of the day. Dad would try to bring me into the conversations because he thought I was old enough to "care about more than myself," as he put it. Zayda had some pretty strong opinions, and he and Dad definitely did not agree on politics, but when the talk got around to other things I was pretty interested in what Zayda had to say. Once, when Dad was complaining about "those lazy hippies," Zayda came to their defense. "They don't understand the world," he said, "but they have good hearts and mean well. This business with the drugs is terrible, but all the talk about love, maybe they're on to something. How can love be bad?" Mom got into that conversation and, let me tell you, it was lively!

At other times Zayda would begin to tell us something, then just say, "Who wants to hear from an old man?"

Danny or I would shout, "I do, Zayd!"

But Zayda would just say, "Nah . . . too long ago."

One conversation I was getting tired of was Dad asking Zayda, "Pop, tell the boys about how you came to America."

Zayda always replied, "They wouldn't be interested." Pop and Zayda had this little conversation about a million times. Exactly the same way. Then one night something

8

happened. Maybe Zayda got tired of Dad asking. Maybe Zayda just felt like it.

Actually, it started earlier in the day. Both Danny and I had gotten in trouble. Danny used a couple of really rude words while doing his homework. You can guess the words. And I had put some smelly, sweaty basketball shorts and socks on the new sofa in the sunporch, and Mom said that the upholstery would never recover and what was I thinking? . . . and where was my consideration? . . . and on and on . . .

So both of us were punished for the day. No television. We played Monopoly and Risk, read for a while, and then sulked until bedtime.

We were just lying in bed, talking about how short-tempered Mom seemed to be lately, when—surprise—Zayda walked into our room. "Walked" isn't quite the word; "shuffled" is more like it. He sat down on the edge of my bed and asked if we would like to hear about when he was just a few years older than I was then and he had traveled across half the world—alone.

Zayda had never come into our room at night, so we were pretty surprised by his presence, let alone his offer. He didn't wait for an answer. He closed his eyes, and, as if speaking in a dream, he just began.

2

Growing Up in Sherashov

"Land!" I could hear someone saying.

I'm still asleep, I think. So I roll over.

More shouting.

Another voice: "I don't see . . . Yes, yes, you are right! Land! Land!"

This is real, I say to myself.

At last . . . after so long.

I jump off the stinky straw mattress, lace up my almost-falling-apart shoes, wrap up my few belongings into a little bundle, and push my way up the ladder with all the other scrambling, stumbling, excited travelers.

The noise! *Oy gevalt*, such noise! And the stench . . .

Wait, boys. I am getting ahead of myself. Let me go back a little. Let me tell you my story from my real beginning, from a world long gone, from a time long past . . .

I was born Meyer ben Yehezkiel in a tiny, dusty shtetl—which is a little village—called Sherashov in sometimes Poland, sometimes Lithuania, sometimes Russia. Wars and czars changed maps; our town stayed the same. The year, I don't know. Maybe 1895, maybe 1896. Who bothered with such information? Let's just say it was sometime after Rosh Hashanah and before Pesach in 5656 by the Hebrew calculations. Neither my papa nor my mama put a star on a calendar on that great day. Maybe Papa made a note in our family's siddur, but I'm not sure.

Papa was a farmer—when the worn-out soil allowed him to be—and a water carrier, and an errands runner, and anything that brought a kopeck or two into our little home. Mama was a slave—a slave to eight hungry children and a husband too-soon old.

We lived in a small house made of wood with, of course, no electricity. We had a water pump right outside our kitchen door and an outhouse in our back yard, because we had no plumbing inside. You know what that means, boys? No bathroom! Mama and Papa slept in one small room. I slept in another with my two brothers; and my five sisters, all five of them, slept in the last bedroom. We ate, read, talked, played, argued, and otherwise lived in the rest of the house, which was the combination kitchen, living room, and dining room. It had a wonderful fireplace. That I remember well.

We had one milk cow and quite a few chickens. It was the job of the younger children to feed the chickens—a job that for some reason I hated. To this day, I just don't like chickens! Eating them, OK, but . . . Anyway, where was I? The outside of the house was unpainted, but every year, just before Pesach, Papa would whitewash all the walls inside.

Whitewash is probably something you never heard of. It's a poor man's paint. I don't know what's in it, maybe chalk and water. But it made the walls look clean after a winter of smoky fires in the hearth, and it excited us kids because we knew Pesach was around the corner when the whitewashing was done.

The street our house stood on was dirt, as were all the streets in Sherashov, if I remember correctly. We lived a block or two away from the shul, where everyone in our neighborhood davened. Well, all the men and boys, that is. Most of the women were too tired, too busy with children, to go regularly, and it wasn't required anyway. I had many friends in that little village, and we were, in some ways, like one big family. I'm sure there were arguments, I'm sure there were fights, and there were people who didn't speak to other people; but my memories are happy ones, of those long-gone times, and I like to remember the good.

From morning till night Mama and Papa worked. From about age three on, we children went to school, *cheder*, and studied long, long hours. Well, I'm wrong. Again, not all of us. We boys went to *cheder*. My sisters helped my mama and learned to cook and clean and sew and mend and garden and do what was expected of them. I can close my eyes right this minute and hear old, white-bearded, round-shouldered Rebbe Schmuel keeping time on his desk with the clopping of a ruler, as he repeated over and over again, "Alef, beyz, giml, daled . . . "

I was a happy kid. My mama was a wonderful cook and our papa told the best jokes and stories. We knew everybody in town and there was always something to do. We played on the edge of the ice and the rushing river in spring, just after Purim, or maybe a little before Pesach. We ran in the tall grass and fields of daisies and swam in that same river in summer. We picked wild berries and grapes and apples at the end of summer and helped Papa make his own sweet, thick wine for the New Year in the fall.

Let me tell you about Rosh Hashanah in Sherashov. It was magic. Right from the beginning of Elul we knew the great Holy Days were coming. There was extra-serious praying in shul, and I remember we added the 27th psalm to our davening. The air was sweet with the ripening apples and pears, not to mention, of course, the grapes that my papa and all the papas were turning into wine! Leaves were turning red, yellow, orange, and brown. Shadows were long by afternoon, and once more we were busy handing down sweaters that had grown too small over the past summer. Every woman in Sherashov was busy—busy sewing a new dress out of maybe a bolt of fabric, but most likely out of pieces of material, perhaps from curtains or even an old tablecloth. Every little house was filled with cooking odors. Some smells, like from honey cakes and *rugelach* and apple cakes, were wonderful! There were also the strong smells of fish baking, onions frying, chicken skins crackling. There were *helzel* and *miltz*, *kreplach* and *knaidlach*. There was *cholent*. There was *petcha*. And *shav*, and *shnecken*. What memories! My mouth is watering! Yup, I was a happy, lucky kid.

In the middle of dark, blustery winter, Mama would make the best potato latkes in the world! We would light our Hanukkah menorah, play dreidel—usually for nuts instead of change—and sing our Hanukkah songs. If we got Hanukkah gifts, I don't remember.

We studied and did our chores and were like children everywhere in the world. We marked the weeks by the glow of Shabbos candles and the seasons by the *yomin tovim*. We fought with each other, we made up, we laughed, we cried, and the years went by. If Papa sometimes read in the paper about troubles in other towns—about pogroms, about attacks on Jews—we didn't worry. We felt safe in Sherashov.

3

The End of Childhood

The world turned upside down on my 15th birthday—
give or take a few months. On that day, as I was walking
home from Reb Yankel the baker, with two loaves of day-
old bread, and daydreaming as usual, I was shocked by
a sudden pounding on the road and a choking cloud of
dust. Before I could get out of the way, a giant shadow fell
across my path and I heard the neighing of a huge, coal
black horse. On the stallion sat a Cossack, one of the czar's
soldiers, as mighty and fierce as his horse and, to me, just
as big. They both had flashing black eyes and wild black
hair. Of course, the horse's "hair" was his mane and the
soldier's was his hat, but what did I know? To this day, I
would swear they both snorted clouds of steam, and they
both bared massive white teeth at me. In my mind, I remember two giants: a giant man and a giant horse. And I
was terrified of both.

The soldier wore high, black boots and a bright red
jacket. At his waist flashed a gleaming, steel sword.

"You!" he bellowed.

I looked around. There was no one else in sight.

"What is your name?"

"Mey . . . Mey . . . Mey . . . ," I stammered.

"Doesn't matter, MEY . . . ," he sneered. "You have 24 hours to say good-bye to your family and report to the center of town. You are now in the army!" And off he galloped, no doubt in search of other victims.

For what seemed like hours—probably more like a minute or two—I stood dumbfounded. This hadn't happened. This was a waking nightmare. This couldn't be real. But then I knew it was, and I raced home, tears streaming down my face, my whole body trembling, my heart pounding in my chest as though to burst.

Now boys, I want you to understand, a coward I am not. I would have gladly gone after adventure. Fighting for something would have been fine with me. Just because I lived in a nice little town didn't mean I wasn't sometimes bored, sometimes restless, sometimes wanting to see more of the world. Of course I did! But this wasn't about a cause, a worthy mission. This was being the czar's dog—worse than a dog, and for years and years, maybe as many as 25 years! This was abuse, insults, humiliation. This was too little, bad food (none of it kosher) forever! And, boys, Russia was not my country, the czar said so. No Jew could be a citizen. But I could be part of his band of frightened kids and hopeless bullies, and for who knew how long?

Mama, Papa, my brothers and sisters, we all knew my choice. Follow orders and die next week, or next month, or next year in some distant, friendless outpost—or run. Leave. Flee that very night. There was no other choice.

Mama's brother—my Uncle David—and Papa's brothers—Uncle Sol and Uncle Dov—all came to the house. There was a lot of shouting, I'll tell you. Uncle Sol shouted, "Send him to Meshel's in Warsaw!"

Uncle Dov cried, "Hide him in Yossi's Tannery, in the storage room!"

Everyone had an idea. Everyone had an opinion. Mama and Papa listened. We all listened, not saying a word. Not even daring to breathe, it seemed to me. I still couldn't believe this was happening to *me*.

"Enough." Papa finally declared, in a slow, determined voice. "No hiding. No fearing the next Cossack . . . or the next meeting, the next terror. Meyer cannot grow to be a man cowering before shadows. He will go to America."

I gasped but said nothing. I looked to Mama, expecting a loud protest.

She only said, "With God's help."

The uncles said, "With God's help," and it was decided. Just like that.

"But . . . ," I started to protest. One look from Papa silenced me. I wasn't a baby. I knew he loved me and wanted me to have a good life. I knew he trusted me, and I was, at that moment, both terrified and proud. And should I lie to you? Excited too!

"Tonight? Right away?" I asked.

"What should you wait for, son?" Papa asked. "For the soldiers to come looking for you first?"

My head was spinning.

Papa gave me the last kopeck he had in the world. Mama tied up a clean extra shirt, my other set of underwear, some socks, a scarf and mittens that she had knit herself, my tallis and tefillin, and my siddur . . . in a little bundle. In another sack she placed bread—that very bread I was fetching when my childhood world ended—a little jar of honey, a piece of smoked fish, and two poppy-seed cookies.

She cried. Papa cried. My brothers and sisters cried. I cried. And I was gone. No map, you understand, just head west, always west. That's what Papa kept saying over and over again; "Stay west, only west, and God will be with you."

4

The Journey Begins

It was almost dark when I set out—my father and my youngest brother, Herschel, going with me for a little way. Then Papa gave me a long, silent hug.

"Stay west," he whispered. "You are a smart boy, Meyer, trust only God and yourself. Try to stay off highways in the daytime, remember your prayers, and don't forget . . . don't forget us."

Another hug, and I could feel his tears on the side of my cheek.

Herschel and I looked at each other, but neither of us could say a word.

My father and brother turned toward home. I just started walking and kept on . . . walking, walking, and walking. I didn't look back. I think if I did, I would have run after Papa, and by now I would be not your zayda, but a long-dead Russian soldier. I was hungry, but I wanted to save my mama's food for as long as possible. I was tired, but I walked on well into the night. Then, with the moon high and the air cool, I stumbled off the road into a field, curled up, and slept. Oh, how well I remember that next morning!

I woke up wet with dew, confused, frightened like you can't imagine. I wanted so much to run home, but west I went, away from the rising sun, toward the unknown.

Luck was with me. Soon I got a ride on a farmer's wagon, and by nightfall I was many miles from home. During the day I ate apples picked up from the roadside, and I shared my by-then stale loaf of bread with the kind wagon driver who had picked me up. He, in turn, gave me a chunk of cheese. He asked nothing, but I am sure he understood why I was a young boy on the road, heading west. My story was not an unusual one in those days.

That night, alone in my "bed" . . . a field, who knows where? . . . I ate a piece of my mama's herring and one poppy seed cookie, salty with my tears.

Maybe you wonder why I had to run, why I couldn't fight for my rights. Well, in Czarist Russia, Jews had no rights. In fact, it was the actual law to make our lives dangerous, miserable, and hard. Official policy. That's just how it was.

And so it went. I walked. Sometimes I got a lift from a wagon driver; sometimes I stayed in a town long enough to earn a bowl of hot potato soup and a night's sleep in a barn. If there was a Jew in town, I could always count on a warm spot in front of a fireplace and a Shabbos meal. Sometimes I stayed in a place for a few days, if there was work. Once, when I met a farmer who was repairing a barn, I helped for, I think, a whole week. But mostly, I just shlepped along dusty and muddy roads, sleeping in fields, eating what God grew on trees and bushes and always, always heading west, only west. I thought to myself, it's a good thing we Jews face east when we pray—that way I know where west is. Always away from the rising sun, always away from my morning prayers.

Was I smart? Was I lucky? Some farms, some houses I just avoided. Some people I avoided. They just gave me a bad feeling and I didn't stop. Some people chased me away as though I had a disease or bad smell, which I probably had. Bad smell, that is, not disease! Some people were kind and generous. In fact, many, many people were, and my life and dreams were saved by strangers time after time.

Oh, there was one time when a bunch of big, tough guys chased me, cornered me, beat me up, called me "dirty Jew," and took the few coins I had in my pocket. I was pretty sore for a few days, with a nasty cut over my left eye. You see this scar, boys? That's my souvenir of that beating— but nothing broken. I just promised myself that I would be more careful in the future, and one good thing came of it: I became an excellent runner. I was never ashamed to run away from trouble!

Eventually I crossed the border into Germany. I had walked many, many miles through what is now Poland but was then part of the Russian Empire. I walked through Lipno and Brzoza, Chelmza and Tuchola, Bialy Bor, Walcz, and a hundred other places. And I learned a little on the road. I learned to stay west, but also north a little, so I would eventually come to the North Sea, from which boats to America sailed. Soon I was walking the German countryside, passing signs to Stralsund, Rostock, Lubeck, Hamburg. I don't know if it was because I was a shy, small-town boy, or what the reason was, but I generally stayed away from cities. I was a little afraid of them, and I thought people would not be quite so friendly or so helpful there.

But now I needed to be at a very important city—the city from which I would eventually sail to my new life. Yes!

At last I came to the great port on the North Sea—Bremen. Bremen was an exciting place in those days. From here I saw my first ocean. Here I saw my first automobile, street lights, modern life! And such bustle, such comings and goings, so many people, and so many boats.

I might have been a country kid who knew nothing of city ways, but I was a good listener and a good watcher. I never lied, but I learned that if you didn't say much, people thought you knew more than you did. So I let people think I knew how to build barrels—and how to shoe horses, and box vegetables, and load and unload boats. And before long, I did know how to do all those things, and I earned. I earned a little here and a little there. I worked long, hard months, growing strong and tough. I must have grown at least three inches, as my pants were now above my ankles and my jacket was a joke, having split across my broad back. But I would not buy clothes, and I purchased only enough food to give me strength to work. Every penny . . . every pfennig, every mark . . . everything I could earn went to only one thing: passage to America.

I was growing big as a man, but I was inside a boy. I missed my home and my family so much sometimes I could hardly swallow—the lump in my throat was so big. But then I remembered what awaited me back there. So I listened to stories of America, and I knew it was worth everything in my life now to save for the Golden Land.

Where did I live, you may wonder. Well, when I first arrived in Bremen I asked some people, please to direct me to a synagogue, a Jewish house of worship. So I found my way to a nice little shul. There I asked if maybe somebody would take in a good, strong boy to do chores in exchange for a place to sleep and breakfast. So I met an old lady, a Mrs.

22

Finklestein, who lived all alone in three very nice rooms. I tended her coal furnace, took out ashes, and ran errands. I guess you could say I became a grandson, and she gave me a warm bed to sleep in and hot cereal every morning. She was a nice lady, and I was sorry to leave her when it was time to go. But she understood, and her kindness was never forgotten, even till this very day!

At last the great day came. How I got to my particular boat is a whole story in itself. When I went to see the United States representative, a fellow in a little office near the docks, I was told about a travel plan that might interest me. It was especially for young men like myself. If I tell you about it now it will spoil my surprise. So you shouldn't mind, I'll just move along and you'll hear soon enough . . .

So where was I? The big moment . . . the big moment was when I boarded the steamship of the North German Lloyd Line—the ship was called the *Rhine*—for the most important journey of my life. In those days, it was not hard to get permission to come here. There were no immigrant quotas. America needed hard workers and the world supplied. So, on a warm spring morning I climbed down into the belly of the *Rhine*, along with hundreds of other hopefuls, and off we sailed. To this day I remember the excitement, the heart-racing thrill! I would like to say I thought about leaving the old world for the new, about home, but, in truth, I did not. I thought only of adventure! Even now, a lifetime later, I get goose bumps from remembering . . .

So soon we were chugging and steaming out to the open sea.

5

Steaming to America

If I ever thought it would be an exciting trip, this voyage to America, I was in for a big surprise. The seas were rough, and the rusty, dirty steamer bounced over the waves like a cork. The accommodations were as bad as the food, and most of us were sick from the first day. We traveled in a class called steerage. Later, when I came to know English pretty well, I realized that "steerage" must come from the word "steer," which is a cow, which is an animal, which is the way we traveled. There were hundreds of us packed like cattle into almost the lowest part of the boat, just above cargo and the boilers—the mighty boilers that burned the coal that made the boat move. Years later, I read that the word "steerage" actually came from the cabin being near where the steering of the boat took place, but I like my definition better. It makes sense to me!

There were no windows in our cabin. There was also no privacy, and "cabin" might be the wrong word. It was one big open area, where families staked out space for themselves. Some strung up blankets to make dividers, but not me. I had no spare blanket, and, since I traveled alone, without a family, I had very little space. It was hot and smelly and noisy, day and night, from the banging and clopping and shoveling and stoking and hissing of all the machinery. Also, I should say, not to mention the crying of babies, the kvetching of children, the arguing of husbands and wives. Noise. Noise. Noise.

For fresh air, we went up long, narrow steps to the lowest deck. Can you picture it? Men, boys, women, children pushing and shoving to get to the railing so we could throw up over the side! And not everyone made it to the rail, either. And for toilets we had buckets, and washing was impossible, and . . . We went on deck to breath sea air and remind ourselves that we were human and soon would be on land. We needed to be reminded. *Oy*, what a trip! Even now I can feel the swaying, taste the bile, and smell the unwashed bodies if I try hard enough.

It lasted less than a month, but felt like an eternity. And how did we keep busy, when we weren't sick? Well, we had plenty of men for a minyan, many *minyanim*—and we prayed! What with morning prayers and afternoon prayers and evening prayers, we were always praising God and begging for a safe arrival. I don't know if everyone was so religious on land, but in that rusty tub—bobbing up and down on the mighty waves of the North Sea and then the Atlantic Ocean—keeping on the good side of God made sense!

Also, one could always find a card game, pick a fight, or practice English. I remember a fellow, Pincus Something-or-Other, about my age, with the homeliest face I had ever seen—no chin, watery eyes, and ears that stood straight out of his head like open car doors. But late at night we could hear Pincus sing, and he had the voice of an angel. All the beauty inside him came out in "Tum-Balalayke" and "Oyfn

Pripetshik," and I don't think I was the only one who shed a tear or two, listening to Pincus, remembering Mama. Hmmmmm, let me see who else comes to mind. There was Leib Haft . . . such a handsome face . . . and Moish Marcus . . . teenagers, both of them, and traveling alone, just like me. Can you believe I'm remembering—I'm remembering these names? I can't believe it!

Music! There seemed to always be music. I think every third person had a fiddle or, at least, a harmonica—what we called a "mouth organ" in those days. You could hear a *freilach* tune night or day.

Oh, oh . . . listen to—

"Deed'l deed'l dye dye . . . dum, dum . . . "

Ah, here's a song that always made me think of home—

"Tum-bala, tum-bala, tum balalayka . . . "

And we always sang—

"Heveinu shalom aleichem . . . "

Now *that's* a melody I still love.

Then there was Chaim Dov HaLevi. I thought he was very old—perhaps 35. He was a small, round man with a bushy, black beard and coal black eyes that looked right through you. He was exceptional. He had been to university as well as the great yeshiva of L'vov, and he knew Greek and Latin, Yiddish, Hebrew, Polish, and Russian. He was studying English by comparing Yiddish and English editions of Shakespeare's *King Lear*. How do you think he made out in America, saying "thou dost" and "methinks" and "forsooth"?

There was Greenberg, a shoemaker, and Weiner, a baker. Weiner had left a wife and children behind. He was eager to earn enough quickly to send for them and already missing them so much he could talk of nothing else. And there were so many others. I see their faces even now . . . even now.

And you could always find a good fight. Such crazy things could start a ruckus! Some know-it-all would declare, "I have it from my own brother-in-law. Abraham Lincoln was Jewish!"

Another genius might say, "The capital of Pennsylvania is Chicago!"

Or, "Fool! You don't put cracker crumbs in gefilte fish!"

Maybe a nervous question, "Do you think they have kosher in America?"

And a shouting match would begin.

Once Chaim Dov told us, "What a strange language is this English. Take the word 'beets.' You make borscht from 'beets.' You can wear beautiful 'beets' around your neck. In the summer, you can sun yourself on the 'beets.' I tell you, it's the same word, means all those things."

We argued about everything—and nothing. And, of course, we worried. And we dreamed.

But now! NOW! We are rushing to the deck—packed like sardines, shuffling toward the ramp leading to shore . . . screaming, laughing, crying—delirious for our first glance of AMERICA.

Should my first sight of America be tall buildings and the busy harbor of New York City? Of course, you say. Here I have a surprise for you. Not every boat that was full of eager new arrivals went to New York. Or even Philadelphia or Boston. My boat's port of entry was Galveston, Texas. Yes, TEXAS! TEXAS, AMERICA!

6

A New Me

About the next few hours I don't have a clear memory—just snatches of this and bits of that. It was completely meshugge in that harbor. I can't even begin to tell you of the activities I saw that day. Ships, boats everywhere—rusty steamers, gigantic cargo ships, big fat tankers, passenger ships, stumpy tug boats, and little fishing boats—millions of them, I thought. Boats loading cotton and grain, so that the air was filled with grit and dust. So many new sights, sounds, smells!

Orders were shouted at us in at least one language I didn't understand at all, one that I had already picked up a few words, and three that I knew quite well. Voices rose up in Yiddish, German, English, maybe Spanish—could have been Italian—definitely some Russian, and I don't know what else. Pure craziness.

"Come here!"

"Go there!"

"Stand in this line."

"Hurry to the gate!"

Scurry, hurry, run, wait, sit, stand, open your bag, shut your mouth, touch your toes, stick out your tongue . . . *Vay iz mir!*

In the middle of this craziness, one inspector was to mark the true, new beginning of my life. He was a big, broad-shouldered man, made taller by his high-heeled western boots, and fiercer by the pistol he wore on his hip. He stood with a translator.

"Name!" he barked at me.

"Vi heistu?" said the translator.

"Meyer ben Yehezkiel. And Mister," I said to the translator, "Dis much Hinglish I'm understandink!"

"What is it—Meyer or Ben?" said the inspector.

"This 'ben,' it means 'son' . . . " I began to explain.

"OK, Benson," he said. "Meyer Benson. Better make it Mike. Welcome to America."

He handed me a document I could not yet read, shook my hand, and waved me on. Meyer ben Yehezkiel touched the soil of freedom, and Mike Benson began his American Dream.

So I am now Mike. Good. Well, a little bit good and a little bit not so good. I am now in America. I now have an American name. But what is this Mike Benson to do? Where is he to go? He still looks a lot like confused Meyer ben Yehezkiel to me!

Like yesterday I see it . . . I am standing in a street. Wagons, horses, handcarts, even automobiles—many more than I ever saw in Bremen! And people. Do you know, here I see my first brown people, Negroes? People, people— swirling around me, and I am standing. Do I go up the street? Do I go down? All looks the same. Nothing beckons. Still not moving, I see a fellow, a *real* American, I think, hurry toward me, hand outstretched. He reaches for my right hand, pumps it wildly, and, with a hearty, booming voice addresses me—in Yiddish!

"You boys understand Yiddish? No? OK, I'll tell you English . . . "*Shalom! Baruchha-bah!*" he shouts. "I am Isaac Weiss, representative of J.I.I.B., that is, Jewish Immigrants Information Bureau, and I can help you."

This country really is a miracle, I think. Yiddish? In Texas? Wants to help me? I accept.

He gathers together five or six of us new arrivals and leads us across the street, down the block, and inside a small storefront office. The office is crowded with many, many people dressed like my Mr. Weiss and some more fellows I recognize from the boat. Mr. Weiss offers us donuts—something new—and fruit. Yup, there sits a bowl of fresh fruit the likes of which I have never seen. Oranges and apples, grapes I recognize, but what is that funny, long, yellow thing? Yes, a banana! My first banana. I reach for one, begin to bite into the skin, when Mr. Weiss gently shows me how to peel it first. We are also offered a choice—coffee, tea, or pop. Pop? What is pop? I know tea. Good enough!

Mr. Weiss sits down at a desk and directs me to a chair across from him. He pulls out a long, official-looking paper and begins:

"Name."

"Mike Benson." New American name!

"Birthplace."

"Sherashov, Russia."

"Father's name."

"Yehezkiel ben Moshe HaLevi."

"Mother's name."

"Tzipporah bat David."

"Date of birth."

"Between first frost and first thaw, 5656."

"Education."

I went to *cheder* in Sherashov from ages three to seven. I was, of course, a bar mitzvah. I can read my alef beyz. A little German. A few words Russian.

"Skills."

"Everything. Nothing. I can learn."

Am I a tailor? he asks me. Would I be wearing such a torn jacket and such silly pants if I were? Am I a cook? Hah! What a question! Am I a farmer? When would I have had any land to farm? What am I? I am an eager, willing *shtarker*. I am a strong back and able hands.

As soon as I say "able hands," Weiss's face lights up. We have an opening on a ranch.

"You'll be a cowboy. Can you ride a horse?"

"Yes!"

In truth, I had ridden only our old dray horse. My papa would put me on his back sometimes, when we returned from milk deliveries, as the nag would steadily make his way to the barn after a hard day's work. And I'd been on donkeys a few times. Never a real horse. But what could be the difference?

Soon Weiss is selling me on the idea of being a cowboy. One, he will buy me the new clothes I will need. Two, I will live in a bunkhouse, which is like a camp, and won't have to pay for rent or food. The ranch will provide. Three, I will be working outdoors, under the bright Texas sky, on the healthy, open range. Four, I will earn three dollars a week.

Three dollars a week! Reason number four becomes reason number one. With that kind of money I will bring Papa and Mama and my brothers and sisters over in no time. Yes! I will be a cowboy!

Mr. Weiss suggests a bath first, then shopping for the clothes I will need as a cowboy. I am a little ashamed, for I know that I must smell terrible from weeks of sponge bathing and little else on that boat. He accompanies me to a bath house, pays the twenty-five cents for me, hands me a towel and a bar of soap, and waits outside. I scrub long and hard and hate to put back on my stinky clothes, but I must. America may be a strange place, but no one here walks down the street in just a towel!

Rubbed red but smelling better, I greet Weiss and we go shopping. First we go to an "outfitter"—an outfitter yet with a Jewish name—Levi Strauss! What a country is this America! From Levi, Weiss buys me clothes like I've never seen. "Levis"—pants with nails? I am confused; "chaps,"—protection against the "brush"— I am mystified; "spurs"—"You'll give a little nudge to the horse," Weiss says. I give up! And more: boots with heels, a very beautiful plaid shirt, a leather vest, a red and white little square of material he calls a "bandana," and then, an honest-to-goodness cowboy hat—a "10-gallon" hat.

I say, "Mr. Weiss, maybe the black one—looks a little more like home."

He says, "Go for white, young man. This is a new world!"

I look in the mirror. A shock. I am seeing Mike Benson, Cowboy, U.S.A! My head spins!

Weiss says, "Let's burn these old, stinky clothes."

My tallis katan—my little undershirt with tzitzis—what I have never been without, is all about who I am and where I come from. This piece of home I'm not ready to leave behind yet. "This," I say, "I'll keep."

We pick up my little parcel—all that is left of my old life: my tallis, my tefillin and siddur, a letter from Mama, and two photos, fading more each day.

While I am becoming a "regular American," admiring myself in every shop window as we walk along the main street, Weiss is leading me to a certain corner where a wagon will pick me up and take me to the ranch. As we stand, waiting, I see Weiss is restless. He has other "greenies" to settle. Do you know what greenies are? A greenie is a brand-new, just-off-the-boat person, who doesn't yet know the ways of doing things in America. I think maybe we were "green" like not yet "ripe," like a green banana or a green tomato. But then again, "greenie" is short for "greenhorn," and I can't imagine how that word came to mean a newcomer like me. Oy, English! What can I say? I'm still learning. Back to my story . . .

I tell him, "Go ahead. I'll wait alone." After all, I had been on my own for a long time now.

He shakes my hand, gives me a slip of paper with his name and address, where I can write if I have problems, wishes me a "mazel tov," a cheery "zayt gezunt," and is off. He is almost across the street when he remembers something. He comes back to me, hands me *ten whole American dollars!* and he says, "How could I forget this? Here is a welcoming gift from Rabbi Henry Cohen, his congregation Temple B'nai Israel, and the Jewish Welfare Society of Galveston, Texas."

I am too shocked to do more than stare back and forth from the money in my hand to the slowly receding back of Weiss.

I stand on the dusty street corner and after a bit I begin to really take in this new country. These streets are paved, but so dusty they remind me a little of home. The buildings are low, one- and two-story; but unlike at home, these narrow houses and stores have fancy fronts and

34

look almost new. They are either painted wood—no house was painted in Sherashov—or made of a stone I do not know. Later I learn the word "stucco," which is not really stone, but like a rough cement—very nice. I notice, also, a beautiful park and flowers. Flowers are everywhere, many flowers like I have never seen. They were gorgeous! They were something else that just amazed and surprised me. I saw flowers in the old country. Naturally I did. But not like these. Such size! Such colors! I think maybe a free land with free air to breath makes flowers grow in a special, Texas way. Of course, the streets that are paved in gold and the skyscrapers, they are in New York, not Texas; but New York can't be too far away. After all, they are both in America.

I feel a little foolish in my cowboy clothes, but as I look around I see almost all the men dressed this way. Of course, I don't see too many straggly beards like mine, but, yes, there are one or two. I must be honest. I called it a beard? Maybe a half-dozen wild, long hairs and a shadow on my upper lip. That was my beard.

I am standing on the street a long time and not one person has said, "Out of my way, Jew." Or shoved me. Or spit in my direction. Men who pass by tip their hats and say, "Howdy." What means "howdy"? Who cares? Soon I tip and say a "howdy" also.

In Europe they call America "the New World." It is *such* a new world to me. I see so many different-looking people. Yellow, white, black, brown . . . different, but the same. This is America!

Hungry I should be by now, but I am too excited to notice. Everything is strange, unexpected. A new life in a new world. Was it only hours ago that I scrambled off that boat?

Some more time passes, and a wagon stops before me. The driver jumps down from his seat, sticks out his hand, and with a big grin says, "You the new hand?"

New name, yes. New clothes, yes. New hand? I don't understand, but I nod.

"Hop in. I'm Luke. From the RVR Ranch."

"Mey . . . Mike Benson," I say, and I feel like I'm talking about a stranger.

"Grab your gear and let's go, Mike. We have a long list of items to pick up before we can set off for home."

So with my "new hand," I pick up my little bundle—now "gear"—climb into the wagon next to Luke, and we are on our way.

7

Luke

First we stop at a large general store. It looks to me like the store sells just about everything, and there are many people shopping on this day. Luke reads from his shopping list, and all sorts of things are piled up on the counter in front of us: sewing needles and thread; a bolt of "nice, mostly blue" calico—which is a material; wire cutters—six pairs; one keg #4 nails; one keg shoeing nails, and so it went . . . on and on and on.

Luke asks if I own a pair of "work gloves," which I do not. He suggests I make that purchase and reluctantly, very reluctantly, I part with $1.25 of my $10. This turns out later to be a very wise purchase. Also, with my own money and at Luke's suggestion, I buy a little block of "personal" soap, my own drinking cup, a notebook, and a pencil. Finally we load the wagon and go to our next stop.

Now we are at a sawmill. This I am familiar with, as I had helped out in a sawmill near Sherashov. We inspect many planks of wood before selecting the ones to bring back to the ranch.

Our last stop was to a "provisioner"—a store that sold foodstuffs. Here we bought several barrels of flour, sugar,

and corn meal. We also bought molasses—something new to me—and, most exciting of all, bananas! How I loved my first banana in Weiss's office! Also, we buy beans. Little do I know that the bananas would go to the family and the beans would be for us cowboys. I would soon learn how much beans would become part of my life.

So we are in the buckboard, on our way to the ranch. As we drive through Galveston, Luke points out the sights: the Rosenberg Library—such a beautiful building of a light-colored brick with much fancy trim; the Texas Heroes Monument with its bronze figure of *Victory*; the new "Galvez" hotel, built by one of Galveston's most important men, Isaac Kempner—a landsman! which means also a Jewish guy; big, European-looking mansions and small, comfortable homes, all light, bright, and sun-bleached. When I comment that everything looks new, Luke agrees. "Yes, most is new, Mike. Only a dozen years ago Galveston was just about destroyed by a great flood. What you see has been pretty much rebuilt since then."

Luke tries to ask me about myself, but I don't have the words yet in English. After a little while we lapse into silence. Occasionally I point to something, ask Luke "how to say . . . ?" And then I write my new word in my new little notebook.

Soon we are out of town, and flat, sandy land lays ahead of us. We drive for maybe an hour or two. The sun is setting and the air cooling. Luke finds a likely spot and tells me we will spend the night here, setting up camp. Sleep on hard earth under the stars? This, indeed, I know how to do!

I gather sweet-smelling sagebrush and twigs. Luke builds a fire. Then Luke puts coffee grounds and water from a canteen into a pot and places the pot over the fire. I help

Luke unhitch the horses from the wagon and feed them before we ever think to feed ourselves.

Finally, Luke unwraps a funny, dried leatherlike thing—I think it is leather—but he laughs and tells me it is "jerky" and to eat it. God is with me and I do not break a tooth as I try to bite into this "jerky" business. I manage to suck and chew it, and you know what? I like it! We also eat fresh, store-bought bread with jelly. And we each have one of the family's bananas. When we travel, Luke says, we're allowed.

My first night in America. I go off by myself a little to thank God for delivering me to this new adventure. Luke glances my way but says nothing. It is a good sign—a good sign that this America is the land of my dreams.

I say to Luke, "It's safe to sleep here? I hear of Indians and wild animals in America."

Luke tells me the fire, which he will "bank" and keep going through the night, will keep animals away and that the Indians in this part of the country have been "relocated." I don't quite understand what that means, but something about it makes me a little sad.

Soon Luke is asleep, and I lie back and look at the stars—the same stars I have looked up at many, many times in my travels from half a world away, and it feels as though I am living someone else's life. Who is this Mike Benson? Where was I yesterday? Where will I be tomorrow? What is in store for this "new" me in this strange, new land? The air is sweet. I am unafraid but very curious—curious about everything! To the unfamiliar sounds of night creatures and Luke's gentle snoring, I finally fall asleep.

The first rays of light awaken both of us. I ask Luke if he would mind . . . I take a few extra minutes? . . . and he says not at all. So I put on my tefillin and tallis and daven quickly, expecting some insult from you-know-who. Luke does look a little puzzled, as though he would like to ask a question or two, but he neither insults nor asks. I am safe in America. I am loving America!

We quickly drink last night's cold, bitter coffee, chew on what is left of the bread, feed the horses and hitch them to the wagon, and we are on our way. Speaking of chewing, Luke gave me a chunk of dark brown stuff that he called a "chaw of tobacco" to chew. Papa used to sometimes put a few harsh, coarsely chopped tobacco leaves in a strip of newspaper, stick the ends together with his spit, twist it and smoke it. He never gave me a taste. This hard-pressed chaw was new to me and, frankly, I didn't like it. I chewed a little to be sociable, but I never got into the habit.

Luke and I try to talk, but I am frustrated by my poor English. I did study on the boat and in Germany whenever I could, and I had picked up quite a few words—but to really have a conversation? Not yet.

We travel two more days this way. When we come to a small town, a town of maybe five or six streets, with one main business street, Luke says, "This is Leggett. We are almost home."

Another hour of jolting along the rutted road and I see a fence, not a proper fence, but a fence made from wire. We drive to a gate in the fence, over which is a sign that reads RVR Ranch. I think, this is it, we are here! I am wrong. We have still almost a half day's ride, Luke tells me, before we come to the heart of the ranch. "Then," says Luke, "we will be home."

8

Home on the Range

Luke pulls us up to a long, rough-looking shed of a building. It is almost dark out and I am stiff from the bouncing ride, but I am all eagerness and curiosity about this ranch.

We have arrived in time for dinner, which is a good thing, because first, I am hungry, and second, it is a good time to meet all the other people. Luke takes me around, introduces me to 10, 20, 50—who remembers how many? Men. Some only boys really. And such names! Juan, said with a *W* sound . . . Pachito . . . Julio, pronounced Hoo-lee-o . . . Man-well. New, strange names to me. I learn later these fellows are from Mexico, and they speak a language I can't understand. There is also James, who came from Alabama, and Yang, who was born in China!

Anyway, we eat. The boys show me around; they tell me they'll "teach me the ropes." This I think I understand. After all, I see each and every cowboy has a rope of his own, and I certainly need teaching to know what to do with such a thing!

Well, this is what Weiss didn't tell me: The "bunkhouse" is a big barn with 20 little cots in a row, on which will sleep

19 sweaty, smelly, snoring gentiles and one confused Jew. The food isn't kosher. From the breaking-in of horses, from the branding and shoeing, from the hog-tying and wrestling to the ground of the cattle—you could get killed! And even the English I learned isn't enough. Most of the "hands," like I already said, speak what I later learn is Spanish.

But I am young, I have a strong body, I am easy-going, and I get along. If the other cowboys make fun of me, I pretend I don't understand. No one threatens. No one tries to do harm. My bed is between a wall on one side and a young fellow by the name of Paco on the other side. At first I am thinking, why do I have such a choice position, a private corner? It doesn't take long to realize that when the wind blows—which is quite often—the sands of Texas come right through the cracks in the wall and I am sleeping on a beach! I quickly learned to take my bedroll and sleep under the stars on warm nights.

Let me tell you now about my new friend. Paco knows as much English as I do, and he knows as much Yiddish as I know Spanish. But slowly we come to understand each other. He is from "South of the Border"—Mexico—and came to Texas to earn money so he could someday go home and buy a little land. I envy him. I could, of course, not dream of going home. I learn of the hard life his family live in Rio Blanco and how banditos roam the countryside, robbing even the poor. I tell him my own story, and we understood each other's loneliness. Pretty soon Paco is saying "Oy gevalt," and I am shouting "Ay caramba!" We both think we are Americans.

To this day I laugh when I think of Paco asking me, "Vos makhstu?" and me answering, "Bueno, bueno."

The food is a problem. Eggs are cooked in lard, which is pig fat. At first I don't eat them. Later I do but I am ashamed.

I feel I am betraying my upbringing. Stews are full of onions and beans and, to tell the truth, taste a little like *cholent.* I pick the meat out and eat. But sometimes, at night, I dream of Mama's *kugel,* Mama's salty fish with white, boiled potatoes, Mama's *hamentashen*—and I am ready to face the czar! Some mornings I wake up early and daven, but, honestly, mostly I forget. I shave my beard. In the Texas heat it is itchy and not much of a beard anyway. Before you know it, I'm a regular cowboy.

Let me tell you a little about being a cowboy. By my time, those rough, tough, shoot-'em-up guys were gone. There were still plenty of cowboys, but we were mostly ordinary, hardworking guys. The wild longhorn cows and mustang horses had been rounded up, and the open range was no more. Most ranches were fenced in, and, instead of long cattle drives, cows took a short walk to the railroad yards, where they rode in box cars to the great processing plants. Many ranchers didn't live near enough to railroads and many didn't want to spend the money for shipping by train, so there were still old-fashioned cattle drives happening.

I was on a not-too-big, not-too-small ranch. Completely apart from the family house was a bunkhouse, a cookhouse, and a mess hall, where we ate. I quickly learned why it's called a "mess" hall. One meal with 19 hungry cowboys and you wouldn't have to ask about the word "mess." What pigs we were!

One time I was sent to the big-house kitchen to ask for some vinegar. One of the boys had had an accident, and we needed vinegar to clean a cut. As I was about to knock on the door, a little kitten ran between my legs and I tripped, fell right down on the porch, knocking over a tub of cream just waiting to be churned into butter. Well, half the cream was on me, and that rotten little kitty was lapping up the rest. Just then a new lady, a lady I never saw before, opened the door and screamed. I was so embarrassed, I began to sputter and stammer and apologize—in Yiddish! First the lady looked shocked, then angry, and then she started to laugh. I blushed deep red under the white cream and continued babbling my apologies. And guess what? She answered me in German. Yes, German!

"Sha, sha," she said. "It's only a little mess. It's only a little cream. Not so terrible. The world she doesn't end." Soon I, too, am laughing.

It seems the strange lady is the new housekeeper, who had just that day arrived at the ranch and who had come all the way from Hamburg, Germany. She was a stout woman, older than me, but not too old. She had beautiful, sparkling green eyes and dark brown hair that she made into two coils over her ears. This was a style very popular in the old country, but not so much here I didn't think. Anyway, her name is Ilsa. She helps me to clean up and promises not to tell anyone what a fool I have made of myself—provided I agree to visit with her from time to time and we should speak German. So Ilsa is another homesick greenie and now my friend.

Well, many an evening after chores I would go to the back porch with Ilsa and Miss Sugar, for that's what we named the kitty. Not exactly. When that animal caused my accident I said, "meshugge" which, of course, means "crazy" in Yiddish. The boys turned Meshugge into Miss Sugar! What do you think of that, a cute joke, no? So Ilsa and I would sit around and we would talk about home. I wonder what became of her. I wonder . . .

9

A Cowboy's Life

It's a rough life, this being a cowboy. A rough life and a hard life. The men, some of them not much more than boys, are hard. They have little patience with a know-nothing like me. I must learn everything quickly and quietly if I am to avoid a fast insult or too-ready punch. I willingly do the worst jobs, just to be accepted. I clean the stables, shovel the manure. I volunteer for just about anything and finally I am accepted as "one of the boys."

Would you like to hear a little about the cowboy business? OK. First I'll tell you about cows. All cattle are called cows, whether a cow or a calf or a heifer or a steer. Even bulls. Texas Longhorns were the most popular cows, not because they were especially good meat—they weren't. They were tough, and those huge horns were dangerous to man and to other cows. But they had one very important quality. They could go for long periods without drinking water. On a drive, being able to do without water for up to four days and nights was often the difference between living or dying. Longhorns were survivors. Also, they seemed to get fewer diseases than other breeds. One other thing, they seemed to handle the

Texas heat pretty well. So that's why Texas is not only called the Lone Star State, but also the Longhorn State!

And something else. It didn't matter if a cow got a little skinny on the way to market. Cows were bought and sold "by the head," which means by the body, not by weight. Even so, we worked hard to fatten our cows on the ranch before the drive because we knew they would lose weight on the trail. And we wanted to make sure they were sturdy enough to survive the drive. The important thing was to lose not even one cow to wild animals or stampedes or accidents. So we cowpunchers, as we were sometimes called, had to be really the super-best at roping and riding, and we even had to be cow doctors when a cow got sick or was having a baby, a calf. And to be a guard at night was especially important because we never knew what might spook a longhorn and set off a terrible stampede! One cowboy was wonderful at calming down a restless herd. I don't know how he did it. He just had a little magic, I guess. Maybe he could talk "Moo"?

I could tell more, but now I go back to my ranch.

My fellow cowboys talk very little—none of them seem interested in sharing their histories. I rope and brand calves with them. I do that most awful, painful job of building and repairing barbed wire fences with them. I do a hundred different chores with them, but mostly they remain strangers to me. Only Paco is my friend.

Let me tell you a little about branding. Our ranch had a long pit near the corral, which was the pen where the cows were kept while we got everything ready. The pit had been dug before I got there, but I had to help make the fire in it. We piled up wood and charcoal and set the fire. It started out with shooting flames, but we waited until there were red-hot coals. At the end of summer, in Texas, being near that pit was hotter than anything you can ever imagine. I sweat a little right now thinking about it!

Where was I? Oh yes, so we had a red-hot pit and we had long irons. Each iron had our RVR brand on the end and a long, long handle. We put the branding end of the iron in the fire until it glowed red. Of course we wore leather gloves. Each calf we would drag near the fire and then two cowboys grabbed him—one by the head, and one by the tail—and threw the calf down on the ground. A third cowboy—sometimes me—would quick as can be put the sizzling brand on the calf's side and hold it for only a few seconds, then take it off. One, two, three—the calf was let go, and a new one was shlepped to the fire. And so it went—hard, hot, smelly, dirty work.

Did I say smelly? Can you imagine the smells—burning hide and cow poop? *Oy*, what a mess. So how is it, boys, that such stomach-churning work still made a person very, very hungry? How is it, at the end of the day, we cowboys fell on huge portions of beef, beans, fatback, potatoes, corn mush, and greens? And we licked our tin plates clean!

This may sound like a terrible thing to do, this branding business. But it was the usual way to make sure which cows belonged to which ranch, because cattle often mixed with others, out there in the open range or on the cattle drives. Every ranch had its own brand and every rancher knew whose were whose. They used to say the animals didn't feel any pain, but I always wondered . . .

I am saving my pay, mostly. When the boys go into town, I go with them. When they drink in the saloon I drink also, but I never really develop a taste for schnapps. I order a shot, play with it, water it down, make it last. I play a little cards, but not much. I don't want to lose my precious earnings, and I'm not so good to win often. Pinochle is my game, not this, what they call poker. The ladies I see do not attract me. They are loud, tough, painted, and old. They remind me not at all of the girls in Sherashov, who would never put makeup on their faces or wear clothes that showed off so much of their arms and chests and legs. Also, I am shy. So is Paco, and we mostly keep each other company. He isn't much older than I am. In fact, none of the ranch hands are. Luke, the foreman—our boss—is maybe 30. An old man, I think! But the other cowboys are mostly in their teens. Living on the range, sleeping in a bunkhouse, caring for cattle is a beginning job, OK for a couple of years, not for long. Not what you would call a "career."

My English and Spanish improve. Still, I am lonely. I am very, very lonely.

I walk toward the sunset on Friday night and in my heart I welcome the Shabbos Bride, but I am alone. I do my chores on Saturday, but I yearn for a minyan, a few words of Torah, being with my own people. Holidays come and go. When, I can only guess. If I knew, it wouldn't matter. Shall I put on a Purim mask in the bunkhouse? How could I make a Pesach seder? Where could I find matzah? To what person could I ask, "Mah nishtanah ha-lahylah ha-zeh me-kol halaylos?" Could I rejoice in Shavuos without holding a Torah or tasting Mama's blintzes? I still have Weiss's address in my pocket. I think I will write, but what would I say? That I am happy? I am not. That the job is terrible? It is not. I do not want to be an ingrate. I do not write.

And so the seasons passed. When I had arrived it was autumn and I was busy learning the ways of the cowboy.

During the winter I spent a little of my precious savings on a very important thing, a sheepskin coat. The winter of my cowboy life was an unusually cold one for Texas and I badly needed that warm coat because one of my jobs was putting out feed for stranded cattle. Where we lived the cattle could graze all year round, but there wasn't enough good grass in winter, so we had to put out bales from time to time. Feeding the cows was hard work. You had to stand on the back of a hay wagon and throw off bales of hay weighing between 50 and 100 pounds each. Can you believe this Zayda was once such a *shtarker*, a big strong guy?

Also in winter we repaired machinery. A ranch back then was a little world of its own. We didn't go to town when we needed something repaired. We had to know how to do everything ourselves.

Even with the feeding and repairing, winter was a slow time for all of us. So on a quiet day the boys and I decided to go to town. What I had discovered was a wonderful, beautiful soda fountain in the drug store. A soda fountain! Can you imagine? What a beauty it was—marble counter and shining brass fizzy-water handles, high stools and a framed mirror behind it. This was something I had never seen before coming to America, and it was here that I had my first taste of ice cream. I loved it! There were two choices, vanilla or chocolate. I have to tell you, I am a "vanilla man." A little seltzer, a little syrup, and some vanilla ice cream . . . Boy oh boy, what a treat! When we would go to town some of the guys would head straight for the saloon. Not me. Why would anyone want burning whiskey when they could have a delicious, sweet, ice cream soda?

Anyway, I am sitting at this wonderful soda fountain when a fellow I never saw before sits down next to me. He is a nice-looking cowboy with intelligent gray eyes and a warm smile. He nods and say, "Howdy" in my direction and gives the soda man his order. What he drinks, I don't remember. What I do remember is his voice. Yes, this stranger sounds like me! I return his "Howdy" and say, "You a stranger in these parts?"

"No," he answers, "I work on a ranch just a few miles south of here."

"My ranch," I reply, "is north."

Both of us are listening to each other and it is clear we are both wondering . . .

"You were born . . . ?" I begin.

"Russia."

"Me too!"

"Town?"

"Sulichowa. And you?"

"Sherashov."

We hadn't the slightest idea of where each other's hometown was, but it doesn't seem important.

Finally, shyly, I ask, "A Jew?"

"YES!"

"Me, too!"

This is a wonderful surprise, a landsman in Texas. And this is how I meet my first Jewish cowboy friend in America.

"Sam Toibin," he says.

"Mike Benson, but my name was . . . ," I begin.

Sam interrupts, "It's a first-class American name," and we shake hands.

Sam, he tells me, he came to Texas a few years ago. He had been a cowboy for five years now, and he loved the life. He loved the adventure, the freedom. He loved animals and the great outdoors. When I told him about my longing for a home and shul in a Jewish community, he told me he did not share such needs. He was happy, for the time being, in the sprawling, wide-open American West that was Texas.

He was in town looking for a fellow who might like to work with him clearing some land. When I told him I might be interested, he took out a piece of paper from his shirt pocket, unfolded it, and read a letter describing the job he had agreed to do—to clear between 50 and 75 acres of mesquite, scrub elm, and post oak. Some of the land had to be "grubbed," which meant roots had to be dug up. Other fields needed only to be cut.

My new friend and I agreed to what I would be paid, and we shook hands on our deal. I spent the next several weeks with Sam, grubbing and cutting and keeping busy during slow season. I also got to know Sam well and very much enjoyed sharing his company after a hard day's work.

When the job was done I lost track of Sam. He had moved on. He was that kind of cowboy, moving from job to job, restless and free.

With the first signs of spring my ranch work picked up and I had little time to think about him. Now I close my eyes and see his handsome, sunburned face and his curious, bowlegged walk.

Spring was fence-building-and-repairing time. And mud time. Everything was covered in deep, thick mud. Also, spring was calving time. Calves were born in March and April. On the RVR Ranch, calving took place on the range and sometimes the cowboys would have to help. All sorts of troubles could develop, and we had to know just what to do!

May, June, and July were such busy months. We cowboys worked hard making sure the cows were healthy and well fed, checking out wells, repairing new holes in fences, clearing thorny brush, doing all the chores we were hired to do. And let me tell you, we certainly needed the protection from our leather chaps and thick gloves.

But now, now it is late summer. All activity is for the purpose of getting ready for the great roundup, and then the great drive to market. What a job this roundup is! Thousands of cows—cows that have been roaming the range all summer—have to be rounded up, counted, made sure they are properly branded, and made ready for market.

I guess the boss liked me, or thought me a good learner, because I was given a very important job: I was made "tallyman." Yes, tallyman. Was I ever proud! I was like king of the cows! I was to keep count of the cattle. I saw who belonged to whom. After all, during the summer, sometimes a fence wasn't repaired quickly enough, and cattle from neighboring ranches got a little mixed together. I pointed out which needed branding and, most important of all, I decided which were fat enough for market. It was my first important job on the ranch, and I was proud and worked hard to do it well.

So now the big event of the year was upon us. The drive to market. I had a choice—I can stay back on the ranch or go on this drive. I had become a good rider of the fast, smart ranch pony I had named Ferd. This was my little private joke. "Ferd" is the Yiddish word for horse. It is also short for Ferdinand, a Spanish name, but I didn't know that when I named my ferd, Ferd. And I was getting better with my rope, my lariat, every day, and once, when I aimed my pistol at a rattlesnake, I actually shot it! Oh, I was some cocky young fellow!

It is hard work, riding long, long hours for hundreds of miles to Kansas City. But I am thinking, "Kansas *City*? A city? Maybe it's big. Maybe big enough to have a few Jews. Maybe even big enough to have a minyan. Maybe even big enough to have a shul!" No, that is just dreaming, but I need to see this Kansas City. I sign on for the drive.

One other thing, as I said earlier, cattle drives were becoming almost a thing of the past. I may never have such an opportunity again, and—let's face it, boys—I am curious and excited by adventure!

I am ready for the cattle drive!

CHAPTER

10

The Cattle Drive

Oh, boys! How can I tell you about a cattle drive? The noise! The dust! That little red and white bandana Weiss bought me saved my life, I'll tell you. Without it over my nose I am sure I would have choked to death. The shouting, the pushing, the circling the cows on my horse! Commotion like you can't imagine. The earth shook, my body shook, my eyes smarted with dust, my throat scratched with grit; and, somehow, in the craziness, order was established, and we were on our way.

A cattle drive is a funny thing. There are moments of real danger—the sight of something to spook the cattle, streams to cross, wild animals to be alert for, storms, tornadoes, lightening, but mostly it is tedious and boring. Keep the cattle moving. Nudge the little stray calves. Rescue the baby caught in a thicket or wandering into a stream. Day after day after day. Sunup to sunset in the saddle; then horses to feed and care for. After that, you drag yourself to the chow wagon and barely have the strength to eat the same dusty stew that you ate the day before and the day before that. But eat you must, to have the strength for the same thing tomorrow. You sleep on the ground and wash hardly at all. A few times after dinner and chores one of the boys would take out a guitar or mouth organ and sweet, longing songs would be sung. Mostly Spanish, because most of the boys were from Mexico. However, James, a Negro, would sing different music. One night, when only he and I were left awake, he told me he was from Alabama and he was looking for a place where the color of his skin didn't matter, and that his mother had been born a slave. I told him it didn't matter to me, and he smiled, but didn't say anything more. Can you imagine that? People owning other people? In all my life such a thing I could not understand. He sang what he called a Negro spiritual, "Let My People Go." What a shock it was to hear James sing about Moses asking Pharaoh to let our people go! I told him how every year we began our Pesach seder saying, "We were slaves in Egypt," and that "Let My People Go" belonged to both our histories. James said he didn't know that and for that little time, we felt very, very close. We two lay on our backs looking at the black sky and the stars until we both fell asleep.

So that's the way it was along the trail. I became brown from the sun and hard from the saddle. I became quick with my spurs, firm with my hands, and good at smelling trouble. I was a real cowboy. On the outside. Inside, I was a lonely Jewish boy. I missed my mama, and I missed the sights and the smells and tastes that spelled home.

The days and weeks passed. We left Texas and entered Oklahoma. The cooler nights told us that we were moving toward autumn and heading north. Traffic on nearby roads increased and farms seemed closer together. One day Luke said, "I reckon any day now we'll see Kansas." Three days later we did bring the cattle, all 4,000 head, in to the sprawling stockyards of Kansas City, next to the belching smokestacks of the processing plants.

Life on the trail was truly hard and the fear of injury or illness was real. There were no hospitals along the way and most remedies were delivered from a whiskey bottle! Fortunately, I never got sick, I don't think. At least, not to remember. I guess if you survive growing up in Sherashov and walking to Bremen and crossing the ocean in steerage and living on ranch food, you are pretty healthy!

I never broke any bones. I did sprain an ankle once, and the boys wrapped it in brown paper and soaked it in vinegar. It hurt but it healed. You will be very, very surprised, I think, by how we treated deep cuts. Are you ready? We made a thick paste out of a chaw of tobacco—tobacco that had been chewed and mixed with a little flour—and we put that right on the wound. Most wounds would heal. Not all, but most. Oh, we had a lot of tricks because there were no doctors on the trail, and if you had to wait until you got to the next city you might be in big, big trouble. Of course, there were some sad stories, but I remember no tragedies on my drive.

You might wonder if we were cowboys like on television, galloping into town, shooting six-shooters, and generally making trouble. Well the answer is, No! First of all, we avoided towns completely on a cattle drive. You can't take thousands of head of cattle for a stroll down Main Street—unless you want to destroy Main Street! Second, we had to live together if we were to get the job done, and most fights were settled with fists if words got out of hand. I never pulled my gun to shoot anything bigger than a pole cat—I missed—and two or three rattlesnakes. One I got. In fact, the one I shot, I kept the skin for a long time, thinking to make a belt; but somewhere along the way I lost it and didn't even think of it all these years until this very minute! I would never aim a weapon at a person, boys. I may have been a cowboy but I certainly still knew right from wrong. How could I forget: Thou shall not murder!

Do you wonder about Indians, boys? Do you imagine your zayda being attacked by bands of painted braves with tomahawks waving? I never saw such a thing. No. By the time I was in the West, it was no longer wild. The Indians had been moved from open land to reservations—special places for them to live—and the only ones I saw were sad, poor individuals, hanging around in towns, often begging. It's a terrible story, boys, a chapter of American history, like slavery, a real *shandeh*—a real disgrace.

11

An Ending and a Beginning

So we brought our cattle in and we were paid what seemed to me a lot of money. I don't remember now how much, maybe forty or fifty dollars. It had been a good drive and we lost no head, so there were no deductions from our pay. You see, back then the cowboys were completely responsible. If we had a stampede, or a terrible storm, or somehow lost some cattle on the way, we would have had money taken from our pay. We heard of some drives where the cowboys ended up owing the owners money! Another reason why drives would soon be a thing of the past.

Anyway, the first thing I did, I joined the boys in a trip to the nearby public baths. Believe me, we surely needed that. Can you imagine weeks on a trail? Can you imagine the grime, the dust, the smell? While we were scrubbing—and I remember we scrubbed several times before the dirt was gone—while we were getting clean, so were our clothes. There were baths and laundries very near the stockyards because every cowboy coming in with his cattle needed those services—and needed them badly!

Finally, squeaky clean, I decided to wander off and check out this Kansas City myself. I left Ferd at a stable and began a long, long walk. After so long in the saddle, walking felt wonderful—and strange!

I walked and walked and walked and finally . . . luck? . . . fate? I came to Sandusky Street—a street of small businesses with names like Rothschild and Sons, Kahn, Heavenrich, Einstein, Hershfield. Could this be a Jewish neighborhood? Then, at the corner of Seventh and Sandusky, I see an actual shul. In fact, a big, impressive shul, Congregation Ohev Shalom. I am just standing on the sidewalk, looking around, not even realizing that tears are running down my cheeks when—fate again? I see a stout, middle-aged man closing up a store and turning toward me. I walk up to him.

"Excuse me, mister," I begin. "Is this by any chance a Jewish neighborhood? Is there possibly a kosher restaurant in town?"

"What would a cowboy want with kosher food?" asks the stranger.

So I tell him my story, and he replies, "The best kosher food in Kansas is only three blocks away—in my house."

And boys, you know the rest of the story. Abe Hershfield took me home. And Abe Hershfield fed my body and my heart. Selma Hershfield ladled out the soup and sliced the pot roast. By the time she had offered seconds of sponge cake and tea I was in love. You know that Selma was Abe's beautiful daughter and your grandmother!

The next few years went by like in a dream. I never went back to the ranch, but I wasn't a quitter. Few cowboys returned from cattle drives. Most just drifted on to another job. I drifted into another world! The hardest thing was saying good-bye to Paco, even though I knew that with his earnings he would be heading for his home in Mexico and, like me, not going back to the ranch. About Ferd I wasn't too sentimental at all. It was time for us to part; but he was a good horse, served me well, and made a rider out of me. I have loved animals—all animals—all my life, since my days as a cowboy.

I went to work at Hershfield's hardware store. When the Great War—what you today call the First World War—broke out, I enlisted and served in France and in Gallipoli—in Turkey—which was the scene of terrible, terrible fighting.

Oh, what I saw there I don't want to think about! I came home in one piece, thank God, though so many good young men did not. And then I courted Selma.

Eventually we were married and blessed with two wonderful sons, your daddy and your Uncle Nate. I worked hard and eventually brought over from the old country my sister Dora and my brothers Herschel and Joe. I never saw my mama and papa and many other members of my *mishpuchah* ever again.

That, my dear Bill and Danny, is the story of Mike Benson, Texas cowboy!

EPILOGUE

It's been many years since those magical nights with Mike Benson. Zayda never got around to telling us about the unusual way he came to America through the Galveston Plan. That story my brother and I had to discover for ourselves when we grew older. We learned how Jacob Schiff, a wealthy and generous man, together with several other important people in New York, felt it wasn't good that Jewish immigrants were settling only in the big East Coast cities. It is true that New York, Boston, Baltimore, and Philadelphia had quite large Jewish populations and immigrants felt comfortable there. But America was a big country and the West was very much in need of hardworking young men. If some guys could begin their American experience away from the usual ports of entry in the East and settle in cities and towns west of the Mississippi, they would be helping to build great new territories, and at the same time they would relieve some of the overcrowding in the East.

So Mr. Schiff created the Galveston Plan. It's a long story—I'll just tell you the basics. The idea was to bring 250,000 Jews over from Eastern Europe. They would be gathered together in Germany, and every boat would sail directly to the state of Texas. The Jewish Immigrants Information

Bureau (J.I.I.B.) helped Schiff and his friends with the organizing. Actually, he had a lot of help from a lot of people.

In Galveston, Texas, Rabbi Henry Cohen of Temple B'nai Israel played a really important role. Rabbi Cohen was a remarkable man who was admired and loved by all of Galveston—Jews and non-Jews alike—for his generosity, wisdom, warm nature, and his caring for people of every race and religion. Even today there are parks, streets, and buildings named in his honor. In fact, it was because of him that Galveston was picked to be the place where these immigrants would first set foot in America!

In 1907, Henry Cohen sent a letter to Jacob Schiff and to Oscar Straus. By the way, Mr. Schiff was one of America's great bankers and financiers; and Mr. Straus was the U.S. Secretary of Commerce and Labor and gave valuable support to the plan. This is what the rabbi wrote: "All western states climate is warm and good. Living is moderate, cheaper than New York. Wages much higher than New York. Population very intelligent and friendly toward Jews."

And so they came, and brought their hopes and dreams, strengths and talents to our great country.

For Mike Benson and Sam Toibin and many others, a first glimpse of America meant the bustling, sun-drenched, southern port of Galveston. They were greeted by representatives of J.I.I.B. and sent to Kansas City and Cedar Rapids and a hundred other little and big dots on the map. Some worked as tailors; some as capmakers. Some built barrels; some repaired shoes. Some worked in the fields and some worked in silver, copper, and coal mines. And a few—a very few—became cowboys!

Between 1907 and 1914, about 9,000 Jewish men and boys were brought to Texas through the Galveston Plan. The outbreak of the First World War ended it, and the plan was never called a success because it fell far short of its numerical goal. However, to the Mike Bensons of the time, it was a great accomplishment. Those 9,000 Jews fanned out from Galveston and settled throughout the West. Eventually they brought their families over and left an important mark on the history of the United States.

One thing you may be wondering, what about girls? What about women? Was this plan only for guys? The answer is: Yes. Women were just not regarded as suitable for working outside of the home. Of course that seems silly today, but this was a long time ago.

Zayda died peacefully in his sleep at the age of almost 100. My brother and I grew up and went on to have families of our own. In fact, Danny has a son Mike, and so do I!

Each Mike is named in memory of his great-grandfather, may he rest in peace. And each Mike's Hebrew name is, of course, Meyer.

One summer, when the boys were quite young, both our families rented a van and toured from Galveston to Kansas City. We tried to picture young Mike Benson arriving in town, going to his first job, riding the trail, and crossing the land. It was a wonderful trip but not at all like Zayda's. Then one night—one black, starry night—Danny and I walked out alone into the prairie and we felt it. We felt Zayda's story in our heads and his spirit in our hearts and we each, in our own silent way, thanked our grandfather for his gift, his sharing his story with us.

I turned to my brother and said, "What a guy, and what a treasure for us—that Zayda was a cowboy!"

GLOSSARY

alef, beyz, giml, daled first four letters of the Hebrew alphabet—the same alphabet that is used for writing Yiddish.

Ay caramba! Spanish, "My goodness!"

banditos Spanish, bad guys.

bar mitzvah Hebrew, the commandment for a 13-year-old boy to become responsible for fulfilling Jewish law. The phrase also refers to the boy himself. Although not mandated by Jewish law, a ceremony to mark this event has become customary.

Baruch ha-bah! Yiddish, "Welcome!"

bat Hebrew, daughter of . . .

ben Hebrew, son of . . .

blintze Yiddish, a thin pancake folded to enclose sweetened cheese or fruit and then fried or baked.

bubbie Yiddish, a grandmother.

bueno Spanish, good.

chaps short for the Spanish word *chaparajos*. Leather overalls or leggings joined by a belt or lacing and worn over the trousers.

cheder Yiddish, a Jewish elementary school.

cholent   Yiddish, a stew made of slow-baked meat, potatoes, and beans, commonly prepared for Shabbos (the Jewish Sabbath).

Cossack   a member of an ethnic nationality known for expert horsemanship and weaponry skills, who fought for the czar in return for land and special privileges.

czar   the ruler of Russia until the 1917 revolution.

daven   Yiddish, to pray, to participate in worship services.

dreidel   Hebrew, a small four-sided spinning top used in a game during Hanukkah.

Elul   Hebrew, the last month in the Jewish calendar before the New Year. It typically bridges the months of August and September.

freilach   Yiddish, happy, cheerful, peppy.

Hannukah   Hebrew, a joyous fall-winter holiday that celebrates an ancient military victory and the rededication of the Second Temple in Jerusalem.

helzel   Yiddish, a chicken or goose neck, stuffed and roasted.

hippies   people in the 1960s and 1970s who rejected the social and political rules of society. They had long hair, wore colorful, exotic clothes, and often lived together in communes. Their slogan was "Make love, not war."

hombre   Spanish, a guy.

kasha varnishkas   Russian, a porridge, usually made from cracked buckwheat combined with little square or bow-tie shaped pasta.

katan   Hebrew, small.

knaidlach   Yiddish, matzah balls, which are soup dumplings made of matzah meal, eggs, and chicken fat.

kopeck   a small Russian coin, similar to a penny.

kreplach   Yiddish, triangular pockets of noodle dough filled with cheese or ground meat, similar to wontons, pierogi, and ravioli.

kugel   Yiddish, a baked pudding or casserole made of noodles, potatoes, bread, or vegetables.

kvetching   Yiddish, complaining.

landsman   Yiddish, someone whose ancestors came from your hometown or country; more generally used to describe a fellow Jew.

latkes   Yiddish, pancakes.

Lone Star State   nickname for the state of Texas. Its origin is unknown but early flags of the republic of Texas, when it belonged to Mexico, show a single star.

Mah nishtanah ha-lahylah ha-zeh me-kol halaylos?   Hebrew, "Why is this night different from all other nights?" Beginning of the Four Questions asked by the youngest child every year at the Pesach seder.

mark   until recently, the basic monetary unit of Germany, similar to a dollar.

Mazel tov!   Hebrew, an expression of congratulations and best wishes, similar to "Good luck!"

meshugge   Yiddish, crazy.

miltz   Yiddish, spleen.

minyan (plural: *minyanim*)   Hebrew, a gathering of 10 men, the minimum number necessary for a religious service according to traditional Jewish law.

mishpuchah   Yiddish variation of the Hebrew word for family—the whole clan, including relatives by blood and by marriage.

"Oyfn Pripetshik"   Yiddish, a song title, "By the Fireplace."

Oy gevalt!   Yiddish, an expression of surprise or a cry for help that means "May a great power intervene on my behalf!"

Pesach   Hebrew, the holiday of Passover, which celebrates the Israelites' exodus from ancient Egypt, where they had been slaves for 400 years.

petcha Yiddish, a jelly made from calves' feet, eggs, and garlic.

pfennig a German coin that was similar to a penny.

pinochle a card game that developed in the United States in the 1860s and is similar to an old French game called bezique.

rugelach Yiddish, bite-size crescent-shaped pastries rolled around a variety of fillings, such as raisins and walnuts, apples, raspberries, or a sweet poppy-seed mixture, and topped with a sprinkling of cinnamon sugar.

seder Hebrew, the traditional ceremonial meal at Pesach.

Shabbos Yiddish, the Jewish Sabbath, observed from Friday evening when the sun goes down to Saturday evening when three stars are visible in the sky. It is a precious day of great joy and spiritual enrichment, spent praying, singing, reading, eating, and resting.

Shabbos Bride Yiddish, a description—often found in Jewish literature, poetry, and music—in which the Sabbath is greeted as a bride or a queen, eagerly awaited throughout the week.

shalom Hebrew, an ancient greeting that means peace, as well as hello and good-bye.

shav Yiddish, cream of leek, sorrel, or spinach soup, usually served cold.

Shavuos Hebrew, a holiday that marks the anniversary of Moses' receiving the Ten Commandments at Mount Sinai and the first harvest of the fruits of spring. Jews traditionally eat dairy foods on Shavuos.

shlep Yiddish, drag, carry.

shnapps Yiddish, liquor.

shnecken Yiddish, little twisted pastries, created by making slices from a roll of yeast dough that has been filled with spices, nuts, raisins, chocolate, or fruit.

shtarker   Yiddish, a real strongman.

shtetl   Yiddish, a village in Eastern Europe before the Second World War, where Jews, usually poor, were the principal or only inhabitants.

shul   Yiddish, Jewish house of worship, synagogue.

siddur   Hebrew, a book containing prayers recited daily, as well as on Shabbos and festival days.

tallis   Hebrew, a prayer shawl.

tefillin   Hebrew, a pair of small leather boxes that contain pieces of parchment on which passages from the Torah are inscribed. They are worn on the arm and forehead by religious Jewish men once a day (but never on Shabbos), usually while reciting their morning prayers.

Torah   Hebrew, the first five books of the Bible, also called the Five Books of Moses, the most revered and sacred book of Judaism.

"Tum-Balalayke"   Yiddish, a popular riddle song that repeatedly mentions the balalayke, a three-stringed instrument played by plucking or stumming.

tzimmis   Yiddish, a sweet, baked mixture of carrots, sweet potatoes, and meat, often with dried fruit.

tzitzis   Hebrew, the fringe attached to the 4 corners of a tallis. Each tzitzis has 608 strands of thread and 5 knots, totaling 613, the number of commandments in the Torah.

Vay iz mir!   Yiddish, "Woe is me!"

Vos machstu?   Yiddish, "How are you?"

yomin tovim   Hebrew, holidays.

zayda   Yiddish, a grandfather.

Zayt gezunt   Yiddish, "Be well."

TO LEARN MORE

If you would like to learn more about Jews in the Old West and about the Galveston Plan, here are some recommendations:

BOOKS

Dearen, Patrick. *Halff of Texas: Merchant Rancher of the Old West*. Austin, Tex.: Eakin Press, 2000.

Dreyfus, A. Stanley, comp. *Henry Cohen: Messenger of the Lord*. New York: Bloch Publishing, 1963.

Freedman, Russell. *Cowboys of the Wild West*. New York: Clarion Books, 1985.

Kessler, Jimmy. *Henry Cohen: The Life of a Frontier Rabbi*. Austin, Tex.: Eakin Press, 1997.

Marinbach, Bernard. *Galveston: Ellis Island of the West*. New York: State University of New York Press, 1983.

Marks, M. L. *Jews Among the Indians: Tales of Adventure and Conflict in the Old West*. Chicago: Benison Books, 1992.

Rochlin, Harriet, and Fred Rochlin. *Pioneer Jews: A New Life in the Far West*. Boston: Houghton Mifflin, 1984.

Slatta, Richard W. *Cowboys of the Americas*. New Haven, Conn.: Yale University Press, 1994.

PAMPHLET

The Jewish Texans. University of Texas, Institute of Texan
  Cultures at San Antonio, 1996.

FILM/VIDEO

Mondell, Allen, and Cynthia Saltzman Modell. *West of Hester
  Street*. Ergo Media, 1983.